GITTA EDELMANN

Zendoodle
for Children

Schiffer
Publishing Ltd®

4880 Lower Valley Road • Atglen, PA 19310

Dedication:

For Anouk, Ben, Dian, Fabian, Inga, Jasmin, Johanna, Julian, Julius, Juri, Karla, Lelia, Lion, Lola, Marie, Matti, Max, Mohammad, Nils, Paul, Timucin, Vianne, Adalie, Carla, Christoph, Clara, Cordelia, Emil, Emilia, Fiona, Friederike, Hyun-Jin, Julius, Lars, Linn, Maurin, Max, Maxi, Moritz, Niki, Oskar, Ronja, Rosa, Séra, Sophie, Tobia, Tom and Viola, and for Gisela and Alexander.

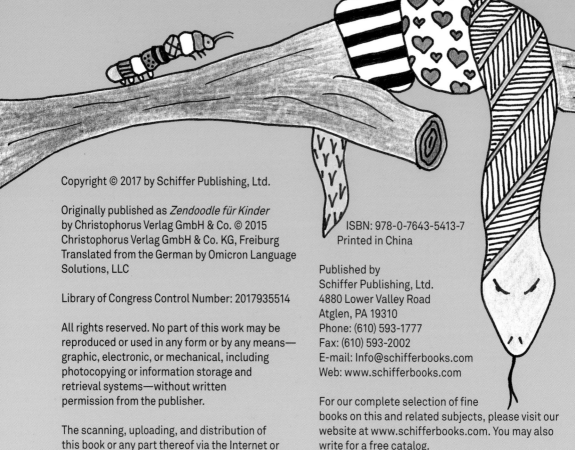

Copyright © 2017 by Schiffer Publishing, Ltd.

Originally published as *Zendoodle für Kinder* by Christophorus Verlag GmbH & Co. © 2015 Christophorus Verlag GmbH & Co. KG, Freiburg Translated from the German by Omicron Language Solutions, LLC

Library of Congress Control Number: 2017935514

Photo credits: Portrait on flap © Gitta Edelmann Layout and lithography: Michael Feuerer Type set in KG Second Chances Solid/Akkurat Pro

ISBN: 978-0-7643-5413-7 Printed in China

Published by Schiffer Publishing, Ltd. 4880 Lower Valley Road Atglen, PA 19310 Phone: (610) 593-1777 Fax: (610) 593-2002 E-mail: Info@schifferbooks.com Web: www.schifferbooks.com

For our complete selection of fine books on this and related subjects, please visit our website at www.schifferbooks.com. You may also write for a free catalog.

Schiffer Publishing's titles are available at special discounts for bulk purchases for sales promotions or premiums. Special editions, including personalized covers, corporate imprints, and excerpts, can be created in large quantities for special needs. For more information, contact the publisher.

We are always looking for people to write books on new and related subjects. If you have an idea for a book, please contact us at proposals@schifferbooks.com.

Contents

Foreword

Do you know Milli and Matti?
They're two mice looking for
the most beautiful patterns.
And you can help them,
by drawing along with them.
You'll see, it's very easy.
Milli and Matti are looking
forward to seeing your patterns!

Zendoodle Tips

1. To Zendoodle is to draw a pattern.
2. Draw with a black fineliner pen on smooth, white paper.
3. Draw slowly so you can draw the lines more accurately.
4. There is no "right" or "wrong." Anything you feel like drawing is fine!
5. Don't use a ruler. Zendoodles are particularly nice because the lines are not quite straight.
6. If you have drawn something wrong—no problem! You can simply continue drawing and pretend that you had planned the pattern that way. Or you can make that area smaller and put a different pattern next to it. Or maybe you can change the pattern a bit right on that spot.
7. Crayons work especially well if you want to color in the spaces. Try using light colors or color very lightly so you can still see the black lines of the pattern.

Milli and Matti Are Looking for the Most Beautiful Patterns

Milli is sad.
The great Festival of the
Animals is coming soon and
she wants to look beautiful.
How does she look now?
Does she look kind of plain?
Does she have any bright colors?
Does she have a pattern?
Milli sighs.

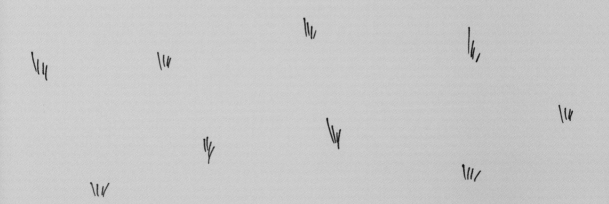

Her brother Matti shakes his head.
"Sighing doesn't help," he says.
"Come on, let's start looking.
Surely we'll find a nice pattern
and maybe even more!"

Milli and Matti meet a zebra.

"You sure are pretty!" says Milli.

"I really like your stripes.

Do you think they would look good on me, Matti?"

Matti nods.

"Sure, stripes are elegant!"

The zebra neighs and grins.

Suddenly a bee flies by,
buzzing around Milli's head.
The bee buzzes, "You know?
There are more types of stripes
than just zebra stripes!
Look here!"
The bee leads Milli and Matti to a suitcase.
"How beautiful!" cries Milli.
"So many stripe patterns!"

A tiger walks by.
Milli and Matti wince,
but the big cat ignores the mice.

Milli begins to draw stripes on Matti.
Phew, that's really hard!
Can you help her?
Yes? Thank you!
Now you can pack your own
suitcase full of stripe patterns.
Have lots of fun!

It is hot and Milli is tired.
She wants to sit under a fern,
but someone is already there.
A frog winks at her.

"Look, here's a new pattern!"
says Matti.
He points to the ladybug
sitting on the fern leaf and
then to a mushroom.
"Dots!" cries Milli excitedly.
Milli and Matti pack dot patterns
in their suitcase. Then they eat
a few blackberries!
Mmm, delicious!

Standing in the soft, green moss, something
glows with colors: blue, green, and purple.
Curious, Milli creeps closer.
"A peacock!" she exclaims enthusiastically.
The peacock is happy and turns a cartwheel.
The eyes decorating his feathers shine.
Now he is even more beautiful!

Matti draws stripes on Milli's ear.
Then it's Milli's turn.
"Would you like a wheel pattern
like the peacock?" she asks.
"Whatever," says Matti.
"Big or small?"
"Whatever," says Matti.
"All of the patterns are beautiful!"

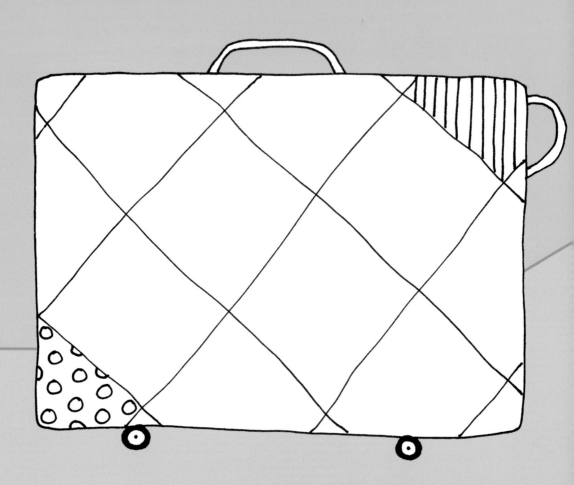

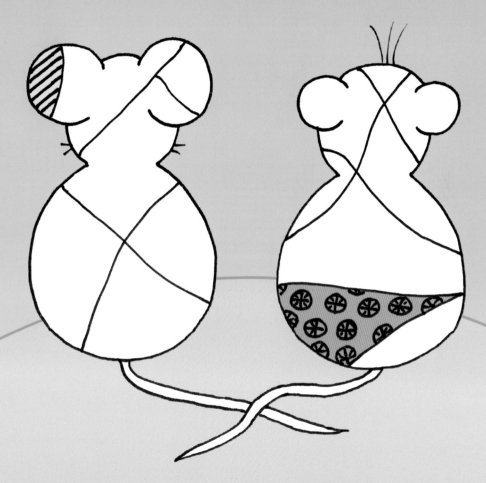

Can you help decorate Milli and Matti,
and help them
pack even more patterns?

"What kind of animal are you?"
Milli looks down from the wall
where she and Matti are sitting.
"I'm a tortoise," says the tortoise.
"And what are you?"
"We are white mice," says Matti.
The tortoise shakes his head.
"I've seen white mice," he says.
"You look different. You're white,
 but you also have patterns."

"Then we are pattern mice!"
says Milli happily,
and the chameleon is happy too.

The mice keep going along the wall.
"A wall like this also looks pretty," Milli decides.
"Let's see what's behind it," says Matti,
 and looks on the other side.

Why, there's a chessboard!
Two black figures are standing next to it.
And there a strange flower is growing—
a chessboard flower!
Matti didn't know there is such a flower.
Milli admires all the new patterns.
"But a chessboard," she says finally,
"Isn't that hard to draw?"

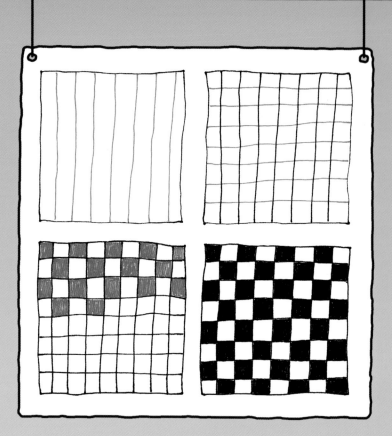

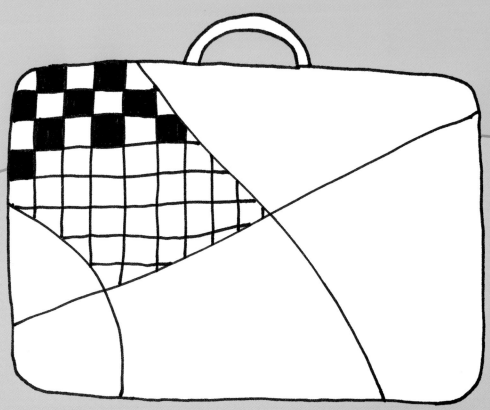

The mice fiddle around a bit,
and then find out how to
draw a chessboard.
Can you do that, too?
Or would you rather draw walls?
Just give it a try!

You can
draw, too!

"We can also draw spots,"
Matti considers,
and looks at the cows in the pasture.
"Oh, yes," Milli agrees.
But the cows do not interest her,
she discovers a different animal!
A really big one!

While Milli draws the spotted pattern,
Matti hears a loud snore.
He looks up.
There, on a gnarled tree branch,
a leopard is sleeping.
"Pretty," whispers Matti,
and points upwards.
Milli nods.
The leopard wakes up, blinks briefly,
and then goes back to sleep.

Why are Milli and Matti running so fast?

They leave their pattern suitcase behind.

"Help!" cries Milli.

"A wild beast!"

"Run!" gasps Matti.

"Polar bears are very dangerous!"

"But wait!" the polar bear calls after them.

"I won't hurt you!"

"Promise?" asks Milli and Matti.

They stand still.

"Promise!"

The polar bear sniffs at the pattern suitcase.
"Do you think . . . " He hesitates.
"Do you think I would look good in
such a pattern, too?" he finally asks.
"I'm always just white—white and boring!"
Milli and Matti look at each other,
and then they nod.

Now Milli and Matti
really have a lot to do.
Can you please help them
draw the patterns?

You can
draw, too!

"Oh, what beautiful spines you have!"
says Milli,
as she meets two hedgehogs.
"May I?"
She pets the hedgehog spines.

"Ow!" she screams
and pulls her paw away.
The big hedgehog laughs
and the little one giggles.
Then Milli pets the hedgehog again,
but this time very, very carefully.

Milli wants to pack the hedgehog
patterns into the suitcase.
But there is a snake in front of the suitcase.
A very long snake.
With its green and yellow scales
it looks dangerous.
But the snake smiles.
"Sssss," it hisses.

You can
draw, too!

The snake says,

"I've heard that you are looking for patterns.

So I stuck a couple in the suitcase for you.

Do you like them?"

Milli nods enthusiastically.

"Then you'll certainly like me also," calls a voice.

Milli turns around.

A crocodile is grinning at her,

proudly displaying his jagged, scaly armor.

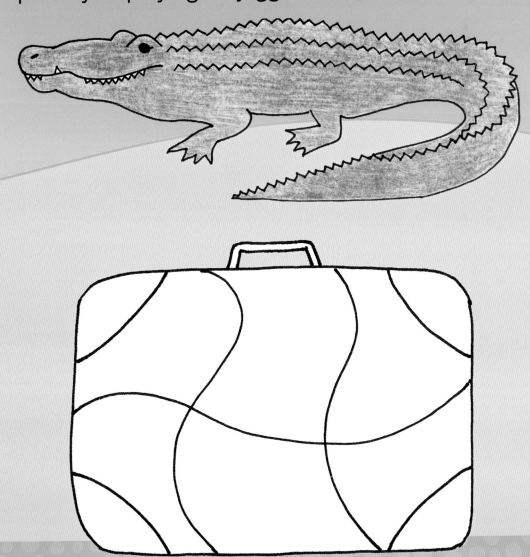

Meanwhile, Matti walks on.
He meets a fat spider that is
just spinning a new web.
Matti likes to watch her.
She is very good at weaving webs.

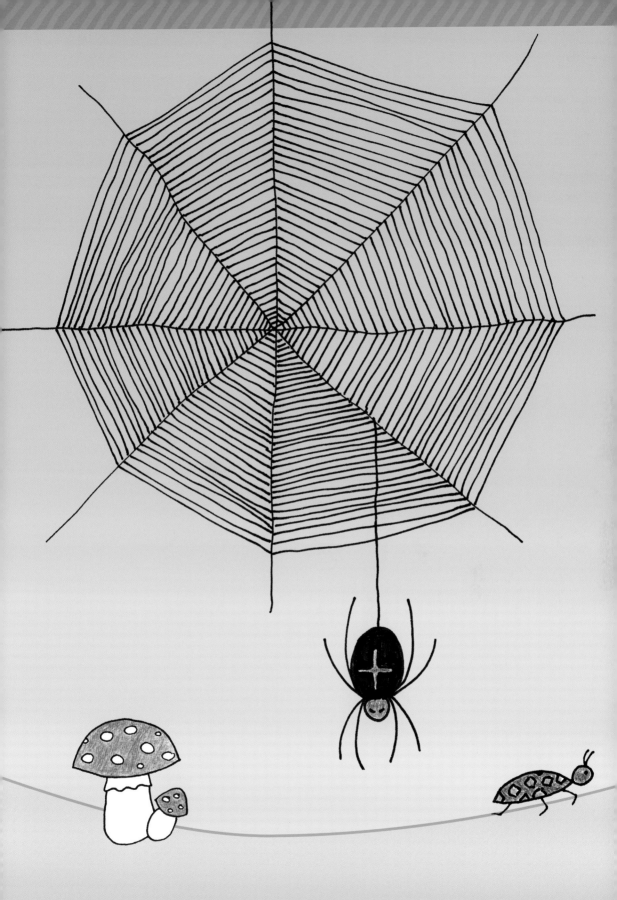

Behind a tree stump,
the mice meet again.
"Look—the tree's yearly rings!"
Matti is happy,
but Milli prefers to look
at how many different
patterns they already have.
Hmm, which one would be the
most beautiful for the
Festival of the Animals?

"The spider web is quite difficult,"
complains Milli.
But Matti has watched the spider
very carefully and knows how to do it.
It's actually quite simple.
You try it, too.
Matti has already begun
a web in the suitcase.

You can
draw, too!

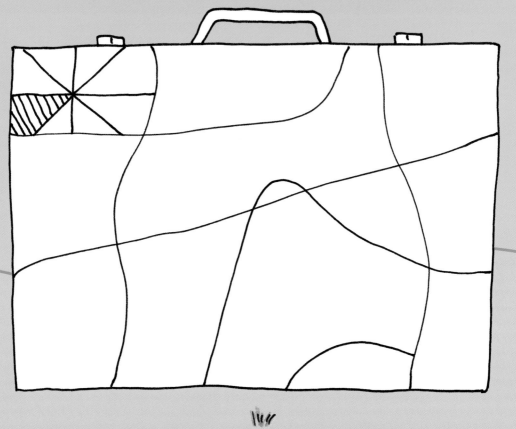

Milli is getting pretty hot.
She walks down to the lake
and lets her tail dangle in the water.
"Hello," calls a fish who is just swimming by.

"Well, you are a funny mouse.
You are not gray, not brown, not white:
you have really strange spots."
Milli smiles.
"I am a pattern mouse."
The fish have never seen a pattern mouse.
"And you're probably a pattern fish," says Milli.
The fish laughs.
"We fish all have scales. Some big, some small.
Do you want a few?"

Milli draws a new pattern on her brother.

Actually, you can draw all kinds of different scales.

And you can even color them in.

Choose a beautiful blue like the fish,

or red or green.

Other patterns look great with scales!

You can create your own Zendoodle.

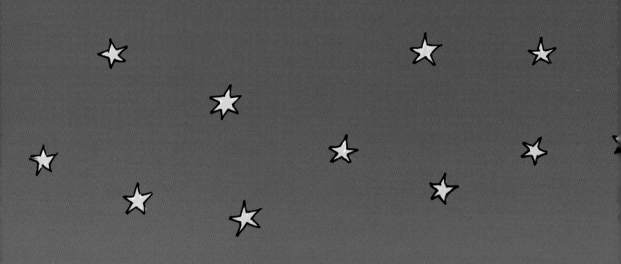

Meanwhile, nighttime is here.
"Look at all the twinkling stars,"
calls Matti as he tumbles around
the flowery field excitedly.
Milli laughs and packs the stars in the suitcase,
as well as the little flowers,
which are growing everywhere.
Then they discover even more patterns:
snowflakes, hearts, and dots.
Beautiful!

In the morning, it is quite windy.
A kite dances in the air. Its tail is fluttering.
"Matti, look!" cries Milli.
But Matti is still fast asleep somewhere.
Instead, a beaver comes running up
and helps Milli draw chessboards,
diamonds, and triangles.
That really isn't so difficult.

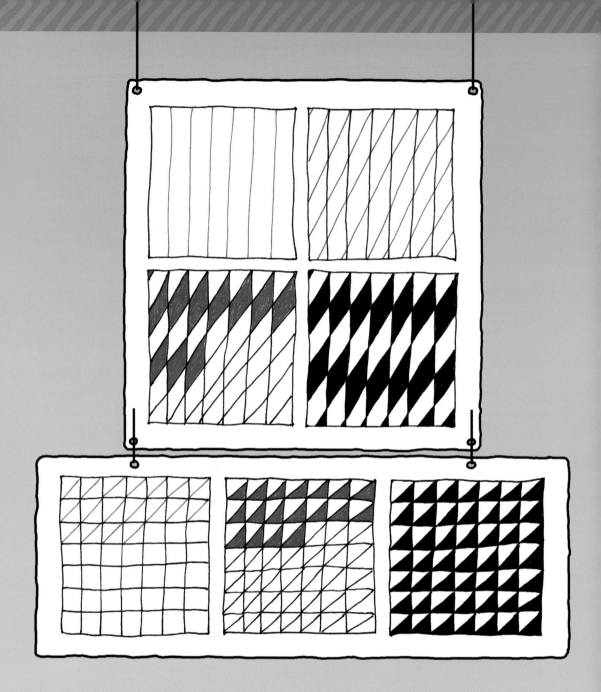

Can you do that, too?
Decorate Milli and Matti
with colorful triangles and diamonds.
Have lots of fun when drawing patterns!

You can
draw, too!

Matti finds a snail already
on her way with her children.
The snail shells shine like
they are freshly polished.
Matti is thrilled.

Try to draw a curlicue pattern!
Or are you thinking of something
completely different?

Milli will be happy
if you decorate her with patterns.

Milli especially likes
the sheep's curly wool.

"Mmm, what smells so delicious?" asks Milli.
"Strawberries!" cries Matti.
He has discovered a whole basket
full of juicy red strawberries.
"Did you ever notice that
strawberries have dots?" he asks.
Milli shakes her head.
"Right now, I am wondering how to
draw a basket pattern," she says.

"Then should I eat the strawberries all by myself?"
asks Matti.
"NO!" cries Milli,
and quickly helps Matti
eat the basket empty.

You can draw, too!

Actually, a basket pattern is very simple,
if you know how, right?
What patterns go well with it?

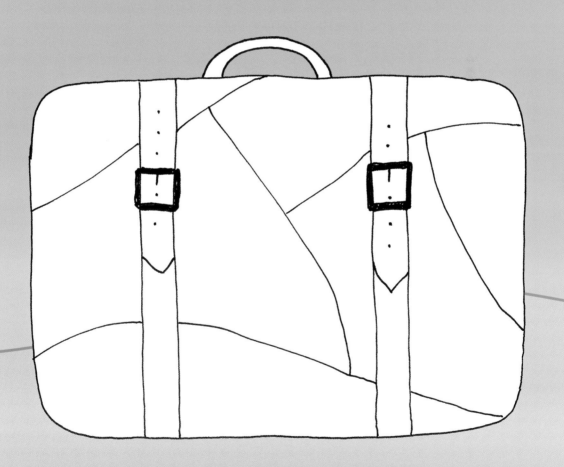

"Who lost this feather?" wonders Matti.
Then there was a loud "Cock-a-doodle-do!"
The rooster hurries up.
"That's mine," he says.
"But if you can use it,
just take it with you!

"Everyone is saying
that you are looking for the most
beautiful patterns," remarks the rooster.
"I'll be glad to help you,
and my hens will, too."
But the hen next to him
isn't interested in Milli or Matti!

Look how well Milli and Matti
have drawn this feather pattern.
The owl likes it. Here you can follow the pattern
step-by-step to draw it yourself.

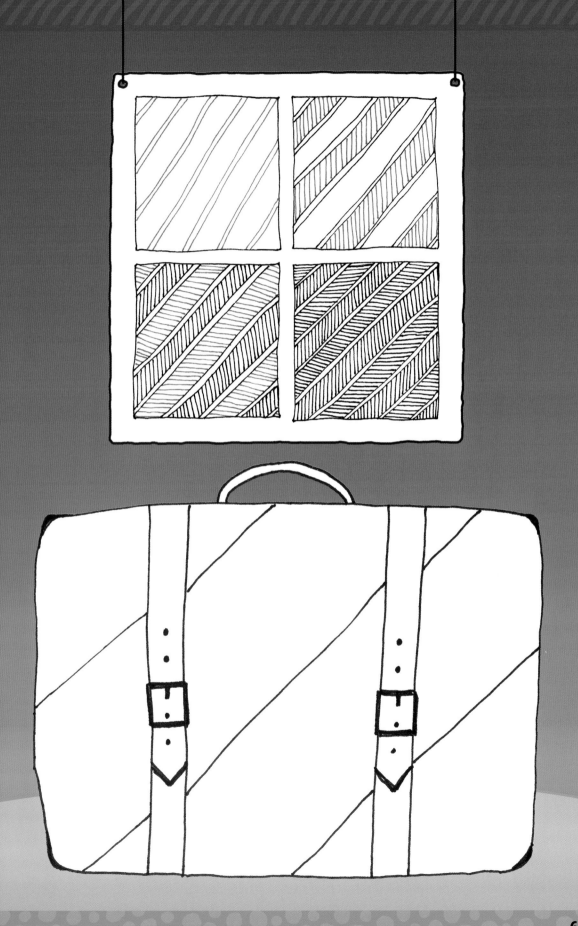

The Festival of the Animals is starting soon.
Milli and Matti make themselves beautiful.
"I still need another pattern," says Matti.
"A really special one."
"I know one," calls a butterfly just fluttering by.
"I learned it from my friend the armadillo!"
And really, the pattern is a very special one!

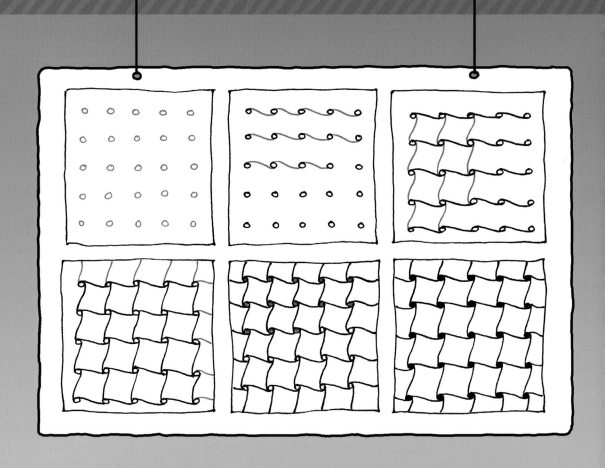

This pattern is pretty difficult, but the armadillo, Milli, and Matti will help you.

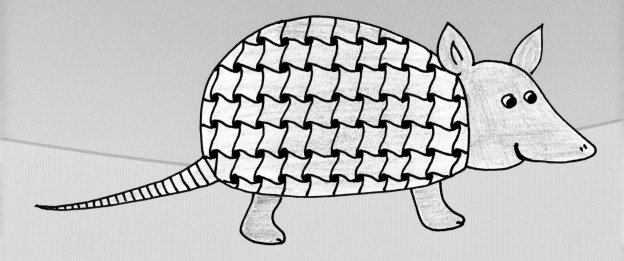

Now let's all go to the
Festival of the Animals together!
Thanks for joining us on the way there!

Festival of the

The festival begins. Everyone has made themselves especially beautiful! Do you see the delicious meal?

SAF

Animals

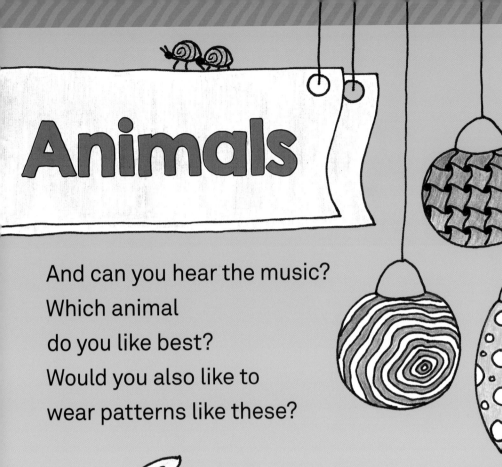

And can you hear the music?
Which animal
do you like best?
Would you also like to
wear patterns like these?

Outline Templates

Which template do you like best?
Enlarge the blank designs with a photocopier
and fill them in with the patterns of your choice.

You can also copy the animals on to colored paper.
Be sure to use light colors, however,
so you can still see the outline of the design.

Or add your patterns to any shape you like:
squares, hearts, flowers,
or even letters of the alphabet.

Have fun!

Meditative Zendoodles
A Treasure Trove of Relaxing Moments,
Susanne Schaadt
ISBN 978-0-7643-5289-8

Bloom
A Coloring Journey,
Diane Kappa
ISBN 978-0-7643-5281-2

Animal Life
Nature Mandala Coloring Book,
Tim Phelps
ISBN 978-0-7643-5278-2

Garden Life
Nature Mandala Coloring Book,
Tim Phelps
ISBN 978-0-7643-5279-9